THE
IMPORTANT
BOOK

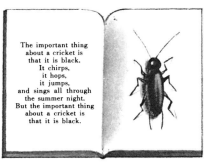

The important thing
about a cricket is
that it is black.
It chirps,
it hops,
it jumps,
and sings all through
the summer night.
But the important thing
about a cricket is
that it is black.

The important thing about GLASS is that you can see through it

THE IMPORTANT BOOK

BOOK

Words by
Margaret Wise Brown

Pictures by
Leonard Weisgard

◼ HARPERCOLLINS*PUBLISHERS*

ISBN 0–06–020720–5.—ISBN 0–06–020721–3 (lib. bdg.)—ISBN 0–06–443227–0 (pbk.)
Library of Congress Catalog Card Number 49–9133
For information address HarperCollins Children's Books
a division of HarperCollins Publishers
1350 Avenue of the Americas, New York, NY 10019
www.harpercollins.com
09 10 11 12 13 LP/WOR 20 19 18 17 16 15 14 13 12 11

The important thing
about a spoon is
that you eat with it.
It's like a little shovel,
You hold it in your hand,
You can put it in your mouth,
It isn't flat,
It's hollow,
And it spoons things up.
But the important thing
about a spoon is
that you eat with it.

The important thing
about a daisy is
that it is white.
It is yellow in the middle,
it has long white petals,
and bees sit on it,
it has a ticklish smell,
it grows in green fields,
and there are always
lots of daisies.
But the important thing
about a daisy is
that it is white.

The important thing about rain is

that it is wet.

It falls out of the sky,

and it sounds like rain,

and makes things shiny,

and it does not taste like anything,

and is the color of air.

But the important thing about rain

is that it is wet.

The important thing about snow is that it is white. It is cold, and light, it falls softly out of the sky, it is bright, and the shape of tiny stars, and crystals. It is always cold. And it melts.

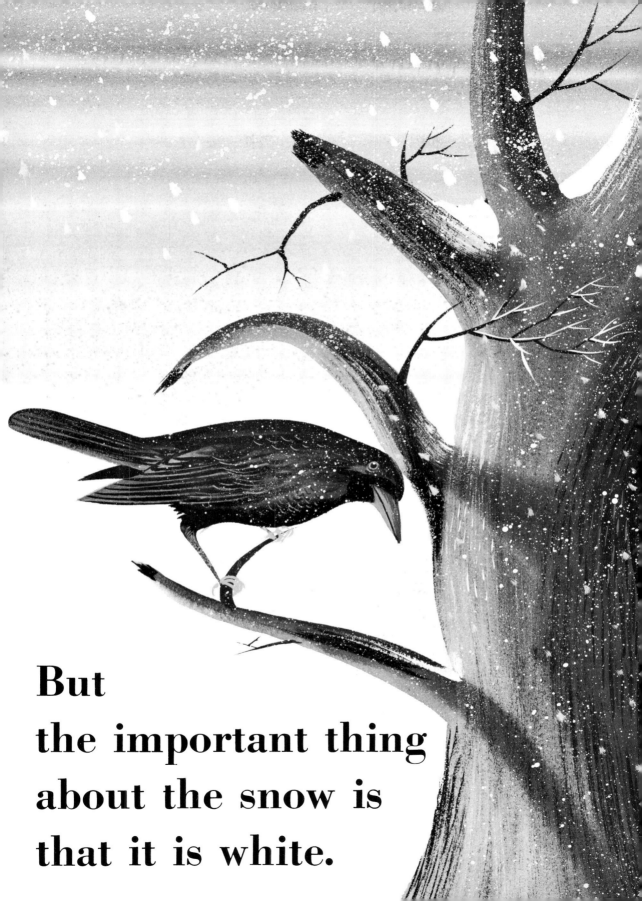

**But
the important thing
about the snow is
that it is white.**

The important thing about an apple

is that it is round.

It is red

You bite it

and it is white inside

and the juice splashes in your face

and it tastes like an apple

and it falls off a tree

But the important
thing about
an apple is
that it is
round.

The important thing about the wind is that it blows. You can't see it, but you can feel it on your cheek, and see it bend trees, and blow hats away, and sail boats.

The important thing about the sky is that it is always there. It is true that it is blue, and high, and full of clouds, and made of air. But the important thing about the sky is that it is always there.

The important thing about a shoe

is that you put your foot in it.

You walk in it.

and you take it off at night

and it's warm when you take it off.

But the important thing about a shoe

s that you put your foot in it.

The important thing about you is
that you are you.
It is true that you were a baby,
and you grew,
and now you are a child,
and you will grow,
into a man,
or into a woman.

But the important thing about you
is that

you

are

you